BAD RATS

by Eric Drachman

illustrated by James Muscarello

Josiah was a rat.

He was a bad rat...or so he was told.

He was sent to the curb, and without a word,
he sat with the others and waited.

Soon, they heard the *tick tick tick* of
toe nails and the sliding scraping sound
of the professor's long leathery tail.

He approached along the curb,
then stopped for a sniff in front of each bad rat.

"Good evening," he began.
"My name is Professor Perimeter, and I will be
your instructor. You are here because of your
behavior problems. You are bad rats...

...but that can be fixed...and I can help."

The girl rat next to Josiah almost smiled when
their eyes unexpectedly met.

"Well well...we seem to have made
friends, already, have we?" asked
the professor with a smirk.

"No, sir," replied Josiah quickly,
"I…I don't even know her name."

Perimeter circled around.
"Then allow me."

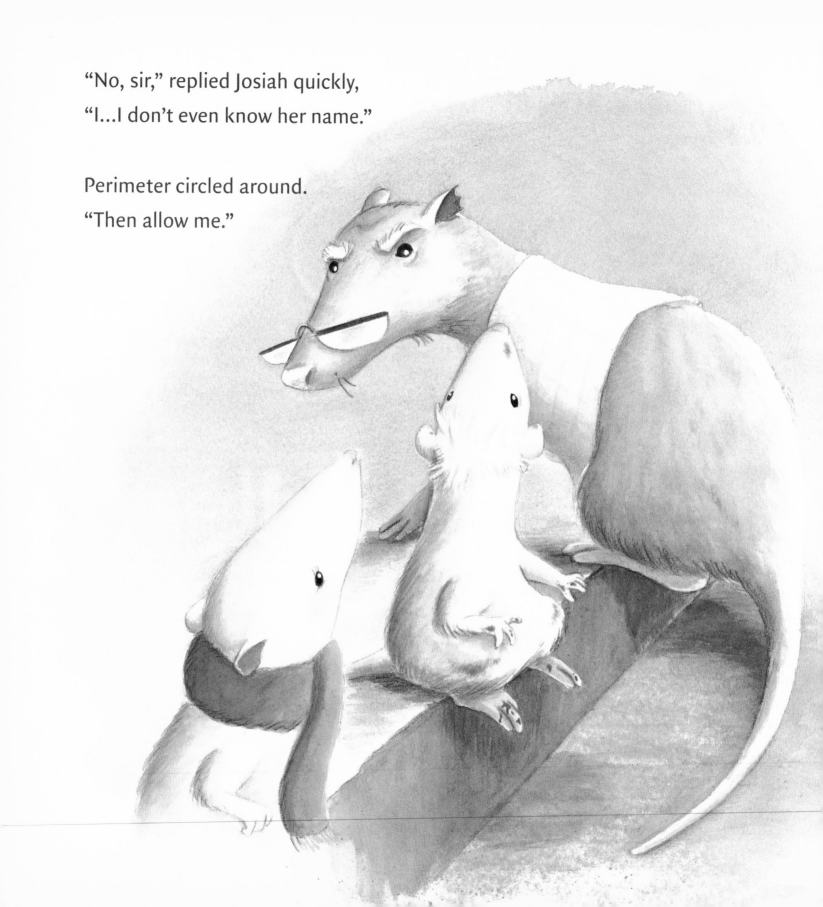

"What is your name?"

"Priscilla," answered Priscilla.

"And yours?"

"Josiah," answered Josiah.

"Ah yes...Josiah, this little diva with the red scarf and a scandalous need to sing is named Priscilla.

Priscilla, this sloppy sloppy boy with the wild hair and a pitiful painting problem goes by the name of Josiah.

I will call you 'Prissy' and 'Joe,' but you will not speak to one another while you are here."

The professor told each rat, one at a time, how they were bad.

"You are bad because you daydream.
You wander away from walls.
You are too thoughtful.
You carry on during the daytime...

...and I believe we even have...a couple of aspiring...*artists*,"
he added, clenching his teeth.

"Wait here," he commanded, and scurried down the alley.

At the dead end, he called out,
"Now walk toward me, all of you."

Halfway there, he started hollering,
"No no no no NO!"

"You must not walk in the middle of the road.
You must not bounce, Sarah.
You must not look around, and
YOU must NOT swish your tail from side to side!"

"You, however, Artemis, were doing very well.
Please demonstrate your technique
for the rest of the class."

Artemis scurried down the alley against the curb

until he was almost out of sight.

"Now walk toward us, Artemis!" yelled Perimeter.

"You see how he hugs the curb? You must stay close to walls.
Keep your tail in a straight line behind you. Look down at the
ground in front of you and don't let your eyes wander.

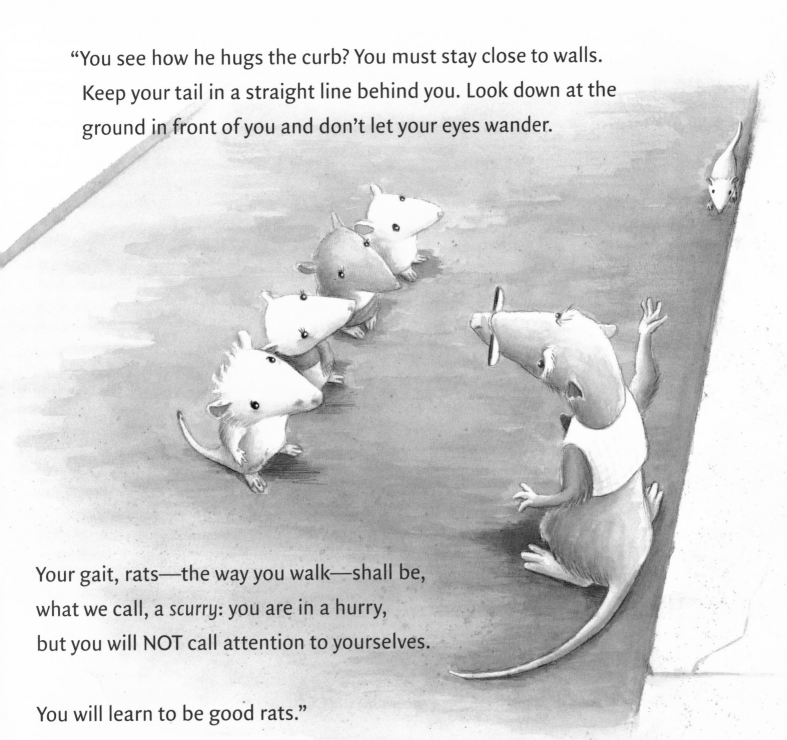

Your gait, rats—the way you walk—shall be,
what we call, a *scurry*: you are in a hurry,
but you will NOT call attention to yourselves.

You will learn to be good rats."

"Nicely done, Artemis. I think you'll conquer that daydreaming of yours."

"Um..." asked Josiah, raising his front paw respectfully, "Why?"

"Why *what*, Joe?" asked Perimeter.

"Why are we bad?"

Perimeter circled the group dramatically.
He'd known rats like Josiah before.

He'd *been* a rat like Josiah, and
rats like him need protection.

"Why are you bad...?" asked Perimeter, leaning in.
"You are bad because you follow your heart
and not your mind. Our minds make
things neat and our hearts are messy.

Your hair, Joe, is all heart."

Turning to the others, he continued the lesson.

"Our minds keep us inside during the daytime,
keep us from wearing brightly colored clothing, Prissy,
find us garbage to eat and sewers for shelter.
Our minds keep our voices low when we find
ourselves in unfamiliar surroundings.

Our minds are what help us survive."

"But Professor," began Josiah, "how would you ever see the color of leaves if you never went out in the daylight?"

"The color of leaves, Joe, has nothing to do with survival. It is for weak rats with big hearts."

"Have you ever seen leaves in the daylight?" Josiah asked.

There was silence as Perimeter
remembered the startling green
of one sunny summer day...

...and how he'd paid for his carelessness.

"Rats!" he commanded suddenly.

"Hurry home before the sun comes up.
I will meet you here tomorrow. Do not be late,"
he warned, and scurried off the way he'd come.

Josiah was confused. *His* survival, he thought, had *everything* to do with the color of leaves. He found some paper and started to paint.

"What are you doing?" asked Priscilla.

"My last painting," answered Josiah.

Not knowing how to help, Priscilla lowered her eyes and headed home, too afraid to push Perimeter.

"I was hoping to hear you sing one day!"
Josiah called after her.

As she continued on, Josiah left his last painting
and walked away...head down, hugging the curb.

The next night, on the curb's edge, they awaited Perimeter's arrival.

"Good evening," he began, and started his lesson.

As he spoke, the breeze delivered Josiah's
painting right up to his very own little rat paws.

He picked it up and quickly lost
himself inside it. He didn't hear
Perimeter speaking to him at first.

"For the last time, Joe, tear up that paper."

"Wh...What?" Josiah asked.

"Tear it up now," he insisted. "It means nothing."

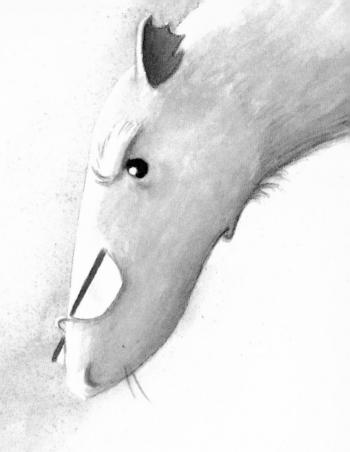

There was no choice. Josiah closed his eyes...
...and held his breath...and...

...and *heard* the most beautiful sound.

Perimeter heard it too, and turned his head.

It came from little Priscilla, but it was not her little voice.

It was a *big* voice, with depth and rhythm and
it made him want to thump his tail in time.

"What's this?" asked Perimeter.

"Her last song..." whispered Josiah, under his breath.

Then Sarah slid off the curb and onto the street. At first, she just swayed to the rhythm of Priscilla's song, and then...

...she *danced*.

"And what's this?" asked Perimeter.

"Her last dance," replied Josiah.

Sarah used the whole street and the curb.
She flowed and jumped and arched in ways that
Perimeter thought were beyond what a rat could do.

It matched Priscilla's voice
and gave it shape...

...and together they found the perfect ending.

Perimeter bent down to Josiah.

"Now show me your painting, Josiah," he requested softly.

The streetlight shone on the picture like a dream, and Perimeter's breath stuck in his throat. It could have meant nothing to him, but just then it meant *everything*.

"How did you know?" he asked in disbelief.

"How did we know what?" Priscilla asked, with her sweet little voice again.

"How did you *see* what I was *feeling*?" asked Perimeter.

"These were things that *we* were feeling, Professor," explained Josiah.

"I see, Josiah,"
Perimeter confessed.

And he did see.
He saw beyond the
walls he'd built,
beyond the world
he'd known, and deep
into the imagination
he'd once possessed.

"You are not...*bad* rats," he managed.

"You're just...

...peculiar.

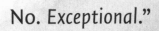

No. Exceptional."

Perimeter breathed...and with a smile on his face,
strolled off in a new direction....

Head up.

Tail alive.

www.kidwick.com

Copyright 2008 Kidwick Books LLC

Voices on CD (alphabetically):
Eli Drachman (Josiah), Eric Drachman (Narrator, Professor Perimeter),
Dalia Piatigorsky-Roth (Priscilla)

Original music was composed and produced by Giovanna Imbesi
at TuttoMedia in Venice, CA. (www.tuttomedia.com)
Roxanne Morganstern (Priscilla's singing voice)
Joel Hamilton (Bass)

Excerpted recordings from *Scherzo* by Gregor Piatigorsky,
courtesy of The Piatigorsky Foundation and Evan Drachman.
Evan Drachman, cello; Richard Dowling, piano.

Text design and layout by Jennifer Adam Wesierski.
Set in Quadraat Sans.
Illustrations rendered with charcoal, ink, and watercolor
on hot pressed watercolor paper.

Printed in Korea
Distributed by National Book Network
Published in Los Angeles, CA U.S.A. by Kidwick Books LLC

Publisher's Cataloging-In-Publication Data
(Prepared by The Donohue Group, Inc.)

Drachman, Eric.
  Bad rats / by Eric Drachman ; illustrated by James Muscarello.

  p. : col. ill. ; cm. + 1 sound disc

Summary: Josiah is a rat. He and his friends are also artists and,
according to Professor Perimeter, painting outside the box is not
very rat-like. These inspired rats teach their professor the value of
creativity.
  ISBN-13: 978-0-9703809-4-4
  ISBN-10: 0-9703809-4-1

1. Rats--Juvenile fiction. 2. Creative ability--Juvenile fiction.
3. Children's audiobooks. 4. Rats--Fiction. 5. Creative ability--
Fiction. 6. Audiobooks. I. Muscarello, James. II. Title.

PZ10.3.D78 Ba 2007   2007902264
[E]